Just Four

By Mary Joyce Zimmerman
Artist: Hannah Putt

Copyright 2005
Rod and Staff Publishers, Inc.
P. O. Box 3, Hwy. 172
Crockett, Kentucky 41413
Telephone (606) 522-4348

Printed in U.S.A.

ISBN 978-07399-2340-5
Catalog no. 2779

3   4   5   6   7   —   21   20   19   18   17   16   15   14   13   12

I'm just a little girl of four;
My name is Mary Ann.

There are some things I cannot do,
But many things I can!

My sister goes to school each day.
  I'd like to go with her;
But she is six, and I am not.
  I often wish I were!

But Mother smiles and says she needs
    A little girl of four,

To clear the table and to take
The cat food out the door.

And then I bring the brush and comb
Out to the "combing chair."

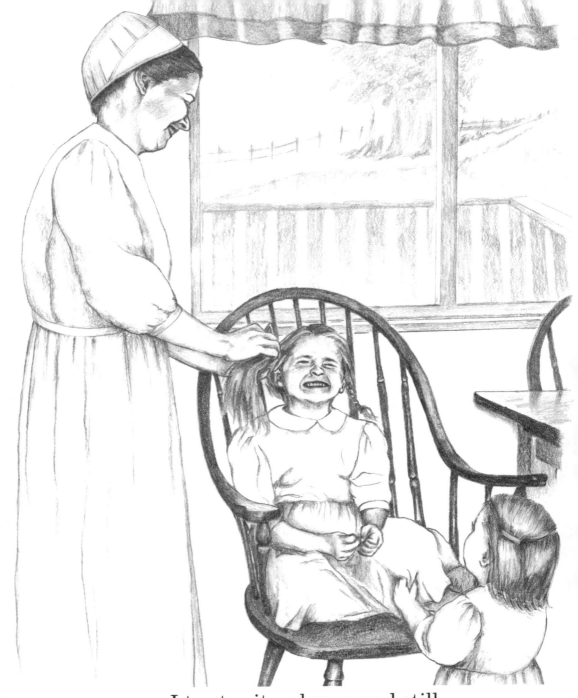

I try to sit so brave and still
While Mother combs my hair.

"That load of wash is finished now."
   And Mother looks about.
"Please baby-sit for me," she says,
   "While I go hang it out."

My little sister looks so sad
When Mother goes, and I

Say, "Catherine, hold my favorite doll."
She smiles and doesn't cry.

Now baby Laura's underneath
The table, finding crumbs.
I try to sweep them with the broom
Before my mother comes.

But Laura tries to grab my broom
'Cause that's how babies do.

She's getting big, our baby is.
She walks a little too.

Then I sit down, and Catherine runs
To get her puppy book.

She crawls up close beside me, and
I page and help her look.

When Mother's finished hanging wash,
   She comes in from the cold.
"Thank you for helping, Mary Ann.
   I need my four-year-old!"

"It makes me happy, Mother dear,
  When I am helping you."
Then Mother smiles. "And it makes me
  And Jesus happy too!"

I ask what makes our hearts feel glad,
  And Mother says to me,
"Our love for God will make our home
  A happy place to be."

Then I help get our dinner on.
And when we're done with that,

I clear the table once again,
And take the scraps to Cat.

Then Mother lets me pick a book,
    And Laura's on her lap;
She reads to us, and then it's time

For everybody's nap.

Some days I am not tired at all;
I must be quiet though.
I get my preschool workbook out
And do a page or so.

Then Mother says I may clean out
The drawer where spoons are put.

There are so many things in there
It hardly will go shut!

I take the things out one by one,
  And then we wipe the drawer.
We sort the things and put them back
  More neatly than before.

And while we work, we softly sing
   A song about God's love.
It is as deep as deep can be,
   And high as heav'n above.

Melinda's home! The door bursts wide;
A gust of cold comes in.

School didn't seem so long today;
How busy I have been!

Melinda asks what work we did.
"We cleaned the drawer—see?"

I peek into her lunch. She left
A cookie—half for me!

Melinda learns a lot at school—
To read and write and more.
And I am learning too, at home.
It's fun to be "just four."